Craig D. Smith

Book of Christmas

20 Poems

&

One Short Story

Craig D. Smith

Requests for permission to make copies of
any part of the work should be emailed to:
Craig D. Smith
CDS.Literary@gmail.com
Or
c/o One-Eighty Films, Inc.
info@oneeightyfilms.com

Graphics Design: Craig D. Smith
Author Photo: Laura J. Tenny
First publication: December 2020

Library of Congress Cataloging-in-publication Data
Smith, Craig D. (Craig Donald), 1949 –

Midnight Pieces / Craig D. Smith
Published, 2020
ISBN: 978-0-578-80019-6
Printed in the United States of America

DEDICATION

For children who bring their
innocence
to Christmas.

Craig D. Smith
Portland, OR
2020

Craig D. Smith

TABLE OF CONTENTS

THE POEMS...

God became a child! But that is just part of the story.

He came to *free* us from the penalty for our rebellion and to *restore* creation. As God made like us, he came to explain Himself to us so we would understand.

This story is not only *mythic*, but it is *true*. In reality, in space, in time, and in verifiable history, a child, born in Bethlehem, God made flesh came to pay on a cross the terrible price we deserve so that dark sin's stain would no longer separate us from God.

And as proof of His accomplishment, Jesus rose from the grave; death will no longer be a final enemy. In Him is the *singular* promise of a restored relationship with God now, and fully realized when He returns again.

Many of these poems were written over the years, a number are new, some are different styles. They and the short story look directly and indirectly at nativity, ransom, restoration, and other aspects at the heart of Christmas. I hope they are interesting and that there is at least one which speaks to you.

For Christmas celebrates not religion but God's love and desire for us, undeserved, graciously offered, and obtained simply by saying "yes" to His gift.

My late wife and I once held each other's hands in the realization of these truths and together asked for His gift to be ours... and that is Christmas!

It makes all the difference in the world.

Merry Christmas,
Joe –
Gary

BOOK OF CHRISTMAS

A Christmas Sonnet

Let me not to truth find impediment.
Love is not love which fails with failure's stain,
Nor gaze which turns away with shaken heart,
Nor looks harsh upon circumstance to change.

No! Love's no faithless sea in churning foam.
In dark, love's still a fixed and endless light,
A constant hope to every wandering soul,
With untallied value; unmeasured height.

Love suffers, even to the edge of doom,
Where God bent down to us, to change our will.
Though sickle, and eternal reaper come,
God's love is constant, and unshaken still.

Surely, love is Christ, the Christmas treasure,
God given for us, is love's true measure.

Craig Smith
Christmas 2016

Upon Advent Borne

We wait for a time, we prepare… and we give thanks.

Listen! Day and night pass us. We are silent and say nothing. Quiet is for this time… and we listen.

Wait! We let go of darkness to know light. What will be is yet out of sight. We bow… and we wait.

Joy! We hope, and look for wholeness. We surrender to do good to others, which is love… and we are glad.

Announce! We will let go of desires. We let go of outcomes. We hold back nothing… and we will reveal.

We wait for a time, ready… and in all things give thanks.

Holiness comes for our souls. We are captured.

Craig Smith
Christmas 2019

A Carol of Winter

You see, it comes each by and by,
In every year it's mirrored.
From midst of Winter's chilly night,
Salvation's horns we hear.

Faint herald of springtime warmth,
That's promised each new May.
This likeness in a simple child,
Who in a manger lay.

A child of rare exception,
A child for dark sin's stain,
A child to bring us back to life,
A child for Kingship made.

And so we bring our kin and kith
'Round table and to hearth,
To think upon this fearsome thing,
To us You do impart.

And O Great Christ, we wait with hope,
And look that day to feel!
When in Highlands and in Coastal Plains,
Then is the curse repealed!

As spring does come each by and by,
By blood His promise sealed.
From midst of Winter's chilly night,
Salvation is revealed.

Craig Smith
Christmas 2002

Ornament

There was no tree, nor holly wreath,
Nor candle burning bright;
Before the one who then was born
Upon *that* Christmas night.

Such trappings were not thought of then,
Just shepherds, by angel's song.
Who saw that day salvation's hope,
For which men with good will long.

A King, a child was born that day,
God Himself, to make us new.
He'd come in flesh to bring us rest,
For nothing else can do.

Now open eyes beyond this day,
And bow before His sight.
To ornament His *matchless* grace -
Upon *this* Christmas night.

Craig Smith
Christmas 2011

Of Him Who is Born for Us
(A Christmas Reel)

Today we come with joyous voice,
These wondrous words to tell,
The Son of God for whom we've ached,
Is born to us today!

Ought we keep this festival,
With pure intent and thankful hearts,
He's taken on our human form,
In Bethlehem He lay.

Jesukin, semper munde,   *(Jesus Child, forever pure.)*
Holy Child, res miranda,   *(Holy Child, most admirable,)*
Jesukin, precious Saviour,   *(Jesus Child, precious Saviour,)*
Born to us today!   *(Born to us today!)*

Jesukin, dwell within me.   *(Jesus Child, dwell within me.)*
Wonderous Christ! Deo datus!   *(Wonderous Christ! God's gift!)*
Jesukin, peace you bring.   *(Jesus Child, Peace you bring.)*
Sound fourth in joyful praise!   *(Sound forth in joyful praise!)*

Call out to the hills!
Shout over the vale!
Proclaim over the seas!
It is He!

Today we come with joyous voice,
To sing of Him and tell to you,
Of Jesukin, our Savior pure,
The flower of Jesse's tree.

Ought we keep this festival,
With pure intent and thankful hearts.
A little child, of heaven's delight,
Has come to set us free.

Craig Smith
Christmas 2003

11

Christmas Grace

Christmas, I'm not afraid of you,
In dwindled embers and ash - or flames.
I remember, other times in your Name...
Snow in our hair, and we all with You.
Now a gift from those little whiles.

This lovely Christmas is lifted now
Beyond the once, that once I knew.
Glowing, quiet and still, and still - full of You.
But better known, and white with hope!
You see, in Truth only - redemption smiles.

Christmas, please linger to hold us well!
Loneliness? At times - it will go, but never far.
And what we miss remains - living! For one is saved...
As Christmas grace still comes, through heaven's door,
To kiss us like a child once more.

Craig Smith
Christmas 2015

Winter's Carol

Awake the heart! And ear and eye!
This day the earth now sings.
For on this cold and wintry night,
Is born the King of Kings.

His birth upon this chilling morn
Besets all natures hand.
As if the harvest time to be,
Came early on the land.

And springtime quickens 'neath the snow,
Impatient are the flowers.
For him to gently call each bloom,
With sunshine and with showers.

But, behold the Savior born to us!
Nature's envy groans this day!
For purposed he, the human heart -
December turned to May!

Christmas 2004
Craig Smith

Christmas Nation.

A Bird on Bellows - a Cuckoo,
A Turnabout Parrot - one, two,
A play Grocers Shop, Aviary,
Toy soldier - a Prussian Dragoon.

A Man Smoking Pipe made of metal,
A Tunbridge Tea Set, three Neat Books,
A Tea Chest and dress'd up Wax Baby,
Parchment Box with a Glass for a look.   *

Gifts joy for each child whispered silent.
Teach truth's fullness held fourth this day.
God's gift come in flesh, Christ a child,
Himself given to take sin away.

To richest, to poorest; feasts are common.
Discharging of muskets in air!
Old Christmas with bonfires burning,
Celebrate carols, we lift voices fair.

Our wish - Christmas time never ending.
A people released by His grace.
A nation of hope, blessed future.
Held sure by His saving embrace.

Craig Smith
Christmas 2014

*   **George Washington gave these Christmas presents
to his children for the first Christmas at Mt. Vernon**

Keeping Christmas

What does one see at the creation of life,
With a birth that makes sure everything?
Are there robes full and golden,
That flow through the sky,
Lit in starlight on celestial wings?

What comes to the ear on that one timeless day,
When the knot of the past is untied?
Is the opus divine?
Does the music ring clear?
As God's provision for sin is defined?

And what is our answer to His touch in our heart?
Is the true meaning of Christmas perceived?
That this Child – God himself,
Took the hurt we deserve,
Not a mystery man could conceive.

May we bow in that light, with joy as a child,
With our stone hearts replaced and now stirred!
For only that change,
Creates life that is new,
And brings hope to a Christmas-time world.

So what can one bring to the creation of life,
On this day measuring sure everything?
That matches the gift,
Set in Bethlehem's heart,
God with us, Emanuel, King!

Craig Smith
Christmas 2013

Saint Brigid Of Kildare

The Bard

The Prayer of the Glen
(A Christmas Psalm)

You have come as a little child.
You have come to my hut in the wood, midst hidden glen.
Outside a tree of apples, a great bounty, huge,
And seemly crop from small-nutted branching green hazels,
Clusters like a fist.

My God has sent it to me, but it is for You!
These and fruits of rowan, black sloes of the dark blackthorn,
Foods of wortleberries, a clutch of eggs and honey,
Produce of heath-peas,
Sweet apples, red bog-berries.
There are herbs, a patch of strawberries; it is for You!

Delicious abundance, haws, kernels of nuts.
A cup of mead from the goodly hazel-bush, quickly served!
With brown acorns, with fine black berries; it is for You!
With good-tasting savor there are pignuts, wild marjoram,
The cresses of the stream – green purity!

Oh, all for You! The glen of fruit and fish and pools,
The peaked hills of loveliest wheat –
The glen of bees, of long-horned wild oxen!

Oh, all for You... the glen of wild garlic and watercress.
Oh, it is all for You... the glen of the rowans with scarlet berries.
Salmon breeding along the rocky stream; it is all *for You*!

You have come in disguise! You visit our hearts.
Is it true You are here as a child?
You have brought the gift and wisdom for which we ache!
All you give us... we give to you.
For you were the one who created the rivers and the salmon,
The nut-tree that flowers!

You are the one who restores all things as a matter of *rare* skill.
Through Your craft comes the kernel.
From You the fair ear of our wheat.
It was You who *made* the bird-flocks.
You *made* the flower of the blackthorn sloe,
The nut–flower on other trees.

Oh a crown of gold shall be on Your head!
You shall have all honey, fresh milk;
You shall have it here with me,
God has given it to me - *but it is for you!*

That I should have a great Christmas feast for the King of Kings!
That I should see the Heavenly Host feast to You!
The great Feast! For all eternity!

And besides these wonderous things,
There is only one greater miracle,
It is that I should be able to be hospitality for your sake,
Here, and in my heart.
For your sake! For your sake!

Craig Smith (adapted)
Christmas 2005

– Adapted from the words of:
  Prayer of St. Bridget, (tenth century Eire)
  & **Tadg Óg Ó hUiginn**, died 1448
  (A member of a well-known Irish family of bards)

Christmas Comes But Once A Year

This Christmas Day through Winter Snow,
Hear bouncing, singing sleigh bells go,
To spread the sound and bid us cheer,
And call the heart to hold friends dear,
For Christmas comes but once a year.

Twine mistletoe in holly wreath,
A favored kiss there felt beneath,
While kindred sip the greatest cup,
Where Jesus Christ is lifted up,
And men the needful message hear –
Yes, Christmas comes but once a year.

Buckram collars, velvet joy,
Gentle candle, waiting toy.
Fiddle dancing, hearts are buoyed,
As songs within us spring.

So quiet now the house is lent,
To sweeter prayers near God's intent,
Which brought to earth His only Son,
To bid men to His person come,
So when it's past, He's ever here –
Though Christmas comes but once a year.

Craig Smith
Christmas 2012

Chantons Noël!

Chantons Noël!
Sing Christmas day!
For here in infant form,
Roi du Ciel!
The Royal Child
Has come from heaven's throne.

Qui nous rend la vie,
As was foretold!
From manger where he lay;
Dieu de majesté,
To us bent down
To wipe our tears away.

Gran mystère!
That He should care
To know our every grief!
En brisant nos fers;
He frees our souls,
And brings us sweet relief.

Chantons Noël!
Hear angels song!
Before Him must we bring!
Nos coeurs pauvres
Our hearts alone;
The treasure of our King.

Craig Smith
Christmas 2010

A Season Silent

In midnight watch
Dark pine trees stretch.
Through frosted air
And icy mist,
Where branches touch
The starlit sky -
Hid from every eye.

Air, crisp and hard,
Blows stinging cold,
And fog keeps
Nothing sharp in shape -
That holds its form,
In dark beyond -
Quiet to human ear.

Echoes – sharp,
In forest white,
The sound of sleighs,
Distant snap of reins.
Hear muffled hooves?
Mid pillars - holy,
And aged-dark,
With boughs of
Sacred green.

These hoof beats pace
Toward brightening gray,
Where phantom bells
Draw even breaths, of deep -
And distant hope, reborn,
That calls to human heart.

Shaped colors bright,
Stained beams extend,
In midnight blackness.
Where songs of light –
A gathered hymn,
Through vale and hill,
With voice resound -
"Alleluia; Christ is born!"

This world, we wait
Through dim and night.
And cold sleep ever
takes our sight.
But steadfast hope,
Bright trusted Truth -
Rings clear each
Christmas night.

Craig Smith
Christmas 2009

29

Oplatki *

We celebrate the birth of Christ
With many symbols deep.
This Crīstes mæsse, His festival,
This joyous time we keep.

For named not so, that long ago
No mere symbol could avail.
But God himself that day bowed down
That hope would sure prevail.

It is that terrible wondrous fact
That measures everything.
And calls to weak and human souls,
That Truth through spirit sing!

In flesh – Nativity, now pressed,
Like Oplatki of old.
We celebrate the birth of Christ -
Reached forth; from hearts made whole.

Craig Smith
Christmas 2008

* **<u>Oplatki -</u> Unleavened wafers, originating in Poland,
embossed with figures of the Christ Child are
given to one another at Christmas with
blessings, forgiveness, and well wishes.**

By Your Leave to Go Across the Sea

Within your bonny eye that day
I saw my loosened fate.
As teardrops merged with misty rain,
Our partin' time grew late.

The cold dreich of that winter day
Brought shivers through my soul.
To ne'er have you near again,
Nor follow where I go.

But every year when Christmas nears
An achin' grace I find.
Though cup be warm, or draught be strong,
Wistful thoughts of you still bind.

I recollect again, that holy day,
My vessel raising sail.
I see you turn as boat departs,
Our duties to prevail.

I treasure now your memory,
As I hae gaen you mine,
We'll meet again on different shore,
Some future Christmastide.

Craig Smith
Christmas 2017

The Day You Came

The day You came,
In some places, there was glimmering snow.
Someone was fishing. A man wiped his brow as he cut wood.
There was a woman somewhere that day - weeping.
A husband and wife sought shelter,
Someone noticed a star.

... A Son was given.
...His name called, *Wonderful*!

The day You came a drunkard was sleeping in the cold.
A king was passing judgment.
There was a child hungry. Somewhere soldiers fought.
A dog barked the day You came.
A leaf fell to the ground,
For some, angels pierced the night.

...A kingdom was established.
...Its power shall have no end.

Midst ordinary things; normal, silent, simple;
Midst life, busy, still, broken and commonplace;
You came! From things grand and stellar,
Things You held together... You came.
We expected lightning, thunder, a sword!
Greater and more terrible wonders!

... But Your name is *Counselor*! Your justice *will* increase!
... Your name shall bring peace, for you are its *Prince*.

Yet to us the weary and the wretched... You came.
Into what the human heart has wrought... You came.
This is the way you came, the day You came!
The Mighty God as an infant child.
It was for us you came... this time... and forever,
For us you came!

Craig Smith
Christmas 2009

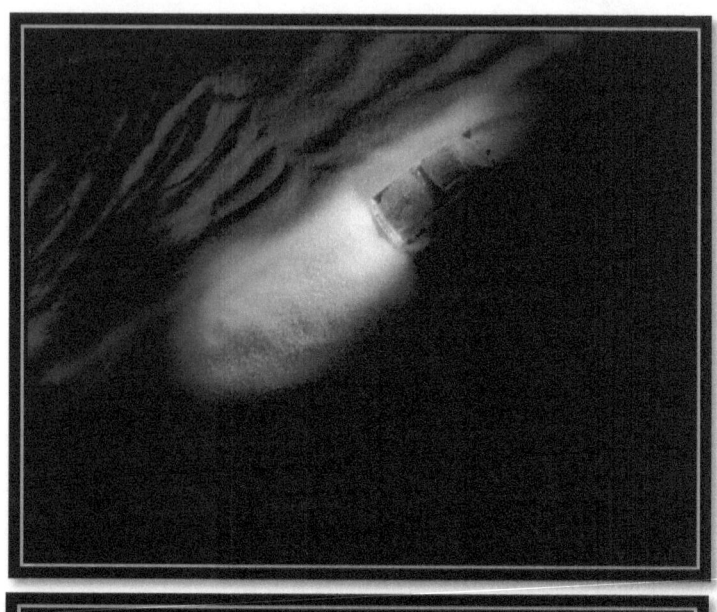

Driving to Christmas

We cross the night time. A midnight frozen world,
Round snowy circles of light clear our shivering pace;
This road, a black knife mark... slicing white cake.

Anxious, yellow eyes grow large, emerge;
But fast behind us, fade to red.

Icy dusts fall and rise in random form,
Wild blinding flecks in wind;
Tiny silver stars that streak across our lonely way.

We drive into this frigid night -
To where Christmas arms await.
Yet pause for a moment... a rest.

Our muffled footprints sound reverently.
And with lights now down... dark descends.
Heaven's reflection reveals itself
In purest glow of true wonder.

Clean, quiet... we speak no words,
And long for holiness.

Craig Smith
Christmas 2017

Nostri Salvatoris

Now let us sing with joy and mirth,
In honor of Messiah's birth,
For he became humanity,
Beneath Angel's reverent song.

With marvelous voice these angels blest,
Poor shepherds and their flocks at rest;
Announced celestial majesty,
From Jesse's tree then born.

As humble as an infant child,
To lie that night in crib so mild,
Where ox and ass did tenderly,
A simple bed provide.

New promised morn beneath His star,
Did draw three Maji from afar,
Met time with tide, the sky had called,
The dawn of Heaven's day.

For in Adam we were all forlorn,
But Christ that day to us was born.
And with his hurt the promise blooms,
Through him true life restored.

Ah! Hear this glorious mystery!
A child! God came! Nativity!
Redeemer, Christ and Lord is He!
We sing of his Noel!

Craig Smith
Christmas 2009

Through the Winter of the World

Sometimes it seems we walk in fear
Through the Winter of the world.
Our faces turned into the rain
To meet a chilly storm.

We see the night is longer spent
With no rest for our pain.
Grim sun does rise in cloudy sky
That but lights our scarlet stain.

Faith and truth that once did guide
With sure and certain way,
Now abandoned like a tinder box
Where cold coals now are laid.

But heaven begs to us below
Take heart and open eye.
For only foolish men hold fast
To things that here must die.

Embrace the Son who on the day
When God turned Self to clay,
Extended hand to every soul
To break the winter day.

Craig Smith
Christmas 2018

Haiku

Christmas snow falling,
White appears on dark pine tree.
Incomprehensible.

クリスマスの雪が降る
しろ あらわる まつ の うえ
私は理解できない。

Kurisumasu no yuki ga furu
shiro arawaru matsu no ue
watashi wa rikaidekinai

Craig Smith
Christmas 2018

Craig D. Smith

Craig D. Smith

ONE SHORT STORY

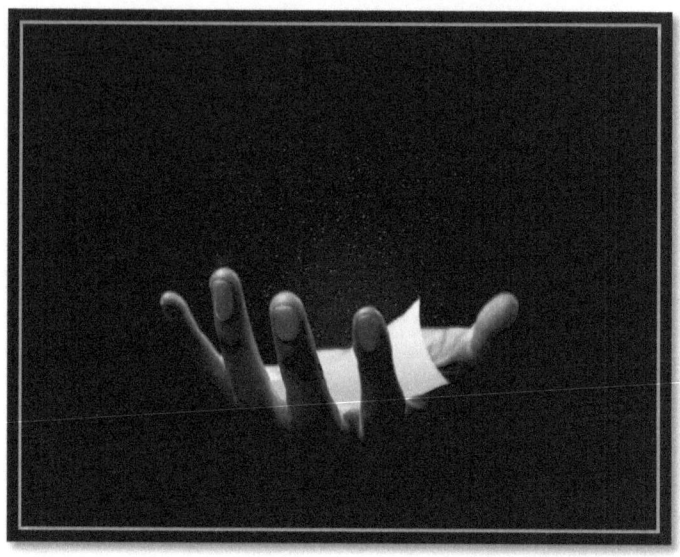

The Final Word

The night was cold. It was a cold that made it hard to breathe. It penetrated thick clothes and all that might wrap a person against it. The wind was like a thousand tiny and piercing blades blowing snow that nipped the face and ripped over the tops of trees. It released great avalanching billows of icy whiteness from laden boughs. It was an unusual storm, with chilly fingers scratching fearfully, almost desperately, at a weathered lodge tucked on a mountainside, a place of gathering.

The lodge stood in a thin scattering of pine trees. It was several miles uphill above a village. In contrast to the fury of the night, the lodge was a warm coal. Its glow came from the families huddled inside and from the heat of a fire in a great stone hearth. Everyone from the village crowded inside. Adults and children were there... all the children, all the families... everyone. No one was left behind. They all came up the mountain in the storm, against its might, up the icy stone path, in carts; some children on men's backs; some struggling as best they could by themselves. The village was empty. All had battled through the storm that raged outside because here in the lodge, here on the mountain... he had arrived.

He had come unexpectedly. He had come like a phantom. He had come as they heard he promised to others; he had come to them as was told he would someday. Now, he was here. He stood before the great hearth. His shadow extended from the firelight, almost as if he were cast into the room as an image from somewhere else. No one knew quite what to expect, but he was here this night, and that is about all anyone cared.

The village below had existed for a long, long time. No one anymore had tried to go much further than the one or two ranges of hills surrounding the great mountain that stood above where the village was tucked. The little community eked out an existence in this particular location. The rest of the world had been silent for a long time.

The village was a refuge. A flow of people had staggered into the town-square over the years. More recently that had ceased. Those who found the town were lost, sometimes half-frozen, broken and starved, always strangely silent with a vacant look in their eyes; all found shelter and help. Those who had come to the village, those who survived, those still alive were here tonight, to see and to hear the Storyteller.

The children had gathered on the floor, crowded toward the glowing fire with clean scrubbed faces. Little and wide-eyed, they stared at the old man, the one who had come, the "teller of the tale" who slowly took a seat on a chair before them. His back was to the warm hearth. However, his eyes sparkled out from the umbra of his silhouette aglow in the frame of the firelight. He was thin like one would expect from someone traveling roads on foot, but he looked strong. That he was old was certain. His white hair shone, and the leathery look of his face made it seem as if he had at one time been a mountain himself, creviced and cracked. But, if you looked at him long, if you studied him, if you paid attention to him, you also noticed something else; something made you realize he might have seen the entire unhappiness of the world.

The gathering began to quiet; the littlest children were especially mesmerized by the man's presence. The adults and older children circled close behind like a protective fence.

Suddenly, a quiet voice, tentatively, broke the silence. "Tell us... now... please," one child plaintively begged, then another, and another until there was a din of small voices pleading.

The man leaned forward in his chair. "You have heard about this story. You may have heard parts of this story but never fully, truly, and never from me... I am the Storyteller. You will hear it tonight, and it will change you... are you ready?"

The children gasped in a din of requests, "Tell us,... please," they begged in tiny voices.

The Storyteller closed his eyes for a moment. They didn't know what the night held, but what it held was why he was here. No one realized, however, the full meaning of his question.

He also knew these children were not as children were meant to be. Many were bent, if not outside, then inside - or both. Indeed, scars and weaknesses were part of the mix of all their lives, both the children and the adults.

For the adults the Storyteller's voice elicited odd confidence. They somehow felt on the edge of a strange finality. Some still remembered. They remembered the world that once was. They longed to release a long weary breath. They hoped over the years that the Storyteller when he arrived, would bring a promise of hope and healing. They needed that for themselves, but even more so for the children in their care. It was a desire that created a palpable and aching hunger that filled the room this night.

"Very well," the Storyteller finally replied to the pleading children, as if yielding by force. "I will tell you the story of the words, but know that once told there will be no going back. Everything will be different."

The men, women, and children stirred. They knew the promise, but how could a story change everything? It shook the fragile confidence of everyone in the room, yet... if they didn't trust, they wouldn't see.

The Storyteller spoke quietly as he explained. "Think... first of all, we have longing to understand things about this world. It is something we feel as a deep desire." He leaned toward the group before him. "Many in the past were waiting like you are waiting. Many understand that things have not been as they *should be. Many hoped for a remedy and wondered like you are wondering right now, 'Can anything change this world?' Many before you also asked themselves, like you are asking yourself right now, 'How could there ever really be something in a story... something so powerful?' You look to me for those answers, but the answer is not from me. This is a story about words that have their own power because they are true words. Truth is something you will finally experience, and in which you will see you need not worry. These words will inhabit your concerns, and you will experience something... extraordinary in their power."*

"Yes... this story, is about words. It is the only story I tell because it is the only story that matters. Many summers, many winters, time gone by, forever past - these words were hidden - no..." he paused, "not hidden, maybe 'lost' is a better explanation. Babies are born with these words on their lips... but they fade so quickly. I know that sometime long, long ago, we all once knew these words. We knew them when all was... younger, when all things were new, fresh, but we stopped listening and lost them somehow. They didn't go far. The words were lost like a coin in your pocket that you forget... then you remember... but it still seems gone. You search further, carefully, and suddenly you find it really never was lost – it was deep in your pocket. It is there!"

Somewhere amid the children, there was a slight ringing. Everyone looked on as a little boy hesitatingly reached down to lift a coin that suddenly appeared near him on the floor. There was a slight shuffling as people turned to each other in whispers.

The Storyteller smiled and continued, "The words were found again. They were found again in winter, and maybe that was just right... it was cold and dark like tonight. A heavy winter had come and spread a coating of white on everything." He stood and walked over to a window. " It could have been in a village like the one down there." He tapped the window and gestured toward the village below, then he turned back. "But really, it has been too long, and some of those details are forgotten. It happened in a year not long ago... but older than a memory."

"The words were discovered, and it was a child who discovered them again." He brought his eyes down to the children. "The child was named Victor, and he was not much older than most of you." The Storyteller smiled as the children found that fact to be something to their delight. "Victor was an exceptional child. That is at least what some say, and that is good enough for this story, all right." He sat down again and rocked back in his chair.

"Victor wrote the words down on something like this." He paused and pulled a small, folded piece of paper from a pocket on the vest he wore. He placed it in his hand and held it out. Slowly, wonderfully it began to unfold itself until it lay flat. "But that they were written did not matter so much as what happened when they were spoken."

There was a rustling in the room as the paper unfolded itself, and everyone began to wonder what mysterious process had begun. Many tried to raise a little to see if something was on the paper. The Storyteller pulled his hand back into the shadows.

"Now these were not new words in themselves, but as far as anyone knew, these words had never before, been put together. Can you imagine... never before! At least since they were originally forgotten and lost."

"Some later said Victor did not understand what he discovered, but I can tell you it is not true. I can tell you that he spoke them first to his mother, four very simple words. His mother told me it was for her as if heaven's door in her heart had opened up; as if stars had fallen from the sky and touched his little paper." The Storyteller gestured from the sky downwards to the page he held in his hand...and oddly enough... there seemed to be a slight glow coming from the paper as he held it out in his palm again.

"They were beautiful words together. They spoke open the dawn of a golden morning. Even though they revealed the human heart and all its error, the four words also kindled a pure fire in the soul which laughed out from a place no one had seen or known since... since... creation."

The children began to nod slowly...silent in their discomfort and agreeing there was something in them never yet totally unlocked.

"And these words spread. Slowly at first but soon more and more, and most people that heard them indeed felt something opened inside, something elemental, magnifying their conscience."

"Why did these words have such an effect?" he asked rhetorically. "No one was sure. Many people studied long and hard and still could not understand. It was just as if an impenetrable door of truth opened to allow a clear and steady gaze inside, and for many it changed the empty place they now saw."

"So what happened to the words?" the little boy in the group, the one with only one arm asked. The old man rubbed his cheeks...children asked him every time... and every time as in the past, he swallowed his heart to the deep secret in its pit.

"What the world now had were words which showed in a true light that this place is as it is not meant to be, and people are as they are not meant to be. Once revealed, the deepest evil slowly trickled in to oppose that truth, to steal hearts and further twist the world. That evil then let in other words and other lies."

"Many resisted, but evil spread like a nightmare. It carried many with it and released a focused fury of destruction. None of us had ever seen the like before... never... in all time, ever," his voice fell. "Never. What

was meant to fly began to crawl until it could crawl no more."

The Storyteller's eyes lowered, and his voice broke slightly. Some of the children began to cry. It seemed to always happen at this part of the story. Such a strange effect; He could feel the children press closer to him. Some began to touch him. Some of these little ones indeed knew the fury of such creatures. Some stumbled as they tried to move. They were wretched and beautiful children hungry for the words, broken and frightened by the world that bent them.

"Don't be fearful," he comforted. "Please don't." His voice fell off. Taking a full breath, he began again. "This all had to be finished, poured out like a bottle that spills out the dregs." He gestured as if shaking out a bottle. "All things are done. All evil is now revealed." As he shook the imaginary bottle, it seemed as if a shadow, a dark and smoky shadow flowed from his gesture to the floor to where it dissipated and disappeared. Everyone nearly gasped at the sight.

"But the words... were they lost again?" A child asked in desperation Others chimed in with honest concern."

"Many who knew the words, many who spoke them were destroyed, not forever, but for a moment," he said. "But another thing happened. After the horrible destruction was accomplished, as some looked and

realized what they had done, as they began to understand they had traded their unlocked soul to follow a heart of darkness. They found they had become deaf... they no longer could even hear the words. Some even say they even turned to stone. Perhaps it's true. I don't believe it, but sorrow and regret was the salt of their tears. They began to fear the power of those words. Because they would not listen, they are gone now forever. All that is left... is you. Now you know how the power of those words had also brought pain."

"What were the words?" a child whispered as the others gasped with wide eyes that he asked such a thing. An innocent request but risky it seemed.

The Storyteller paused for a long moment. The ritual had begun as he had seen it before. He leaned forward as the children held their breath, "I am just the Storyteller... but these are the words." As the adults watched they suddenly realized the words were on his tongue.

Before anyone could stop him, he spoke them... the terrible, the beautiful words.

The children, the adults... the words had their effect... they flooded into their hearts, and they began to weep bitterly as if stabbed by some unseen knife. For them, it was now the agony of realization that endings and pain had not come from just a bottle of shadows, but from the shadow of a divided heart. That, while having the untouchable good at their grasp, they could so easily embrace darkness. They had seen it, resisted it, but they now saw how fearfully available it still was inside themselves.

The Storyteller leaned back in his chair. His extraordinary eyes seemed to hold some secret yet unrevealed. "Oh children, everyone, don't worry... you now see fully... but know... those words are not complete." He began to move closer to the children.

"They should be lost!" one child said in tears. "We should forget them forever," he said fearfully. But another child, whose legs were twisted with the wickedness he had endured, struggled to move among the group of children with a new question. "What happened to Victor?"

The man settled the children and rocked back, breathing deeply. He smiled and looked directly at everyone with an odd silence. Suddenly they could see... they realized, and they knew who the Storyteller was.

This was no ordinary night. It was something beyond their expectations. The Storyteller spoke, "Victor alone was finally given the real truth of the words, those mysterious words. Few were ready for the secret."

The room became silent as an empty cradle. The fire had dimmed, but its flickering light painted all the faces. Hearts were now afire as the Storyteller leaned from the darkness towards his listeners. "The secret is that there is another word to be known, a final word. It was given to Victor to tell."

The fire suddenly crackled and flashed, sending out red sparks over the hearth. No one moved. The group was his now... not their own. There was not a sound from them... all words had all been spoken...used... except for one. The only sound in the little space was the breath of their beings rattling their inner chains because hope was still wingless.

The Storyteller now took a deep breath and looked around the room with haunting black eyes, "First you must listen to know and understand the words given to you are true. They are true, and they are really... the beginning words." The old man then spoke the four words once more... only this time, somehow... differently.

Suddenly, the room began to glow and slowly fill with a strange and wonderful light... a light of the rainbows of paradise! The Storyteller now was smiling. He began to laugh, and he looked like he was growing... younger. He was changing. His youth was being restored before their eyes!

But something was also happening to the adults. The inner echoes of the children they were at one time began to return. Some distant, unrealized past that was engulfed by their weary years was fleeing. A cold burden was lifting. Something marvelous was happening. Could it be? Somehow, their youth was being restored. They were becoming children in the same way as the teller of the story!

Joy now broke into the gathering like a powerful sunshine. It rang, pealing and swelling like the singing of bells. It spread a golden thickness of soft caresses across all faces. Hurt and fear melted from every eye. Wounds and scars were erased. The room was being made whole and becoming filled... with children.

All looked in wonder as the four words stopped playing in their ears. The face of the Storyteller seemed to be shining with a fearsome and indescribable kindness. There would be finality... protection was in truth. Coming here to the lodge they all had felt a strange new dawn was near, but it was a dawn that had no words – no color, no music. They all now resonated with the words of heaven. How could they have not noticed and seen? How could they not have trusted so much more fully until now?

Masked no longer, the Storyteller leaned closer and spoke as if he was whispering in each ear in the room. "And this, little children, is the word that holds more power than all before. It is the last. It is the restoration word. It is the word that will change the world forever. It is the explanation word... it is..." he paused, "... the final word."

And he spoke the word softly.

There was a small but firm... rumble!

Nothing would be the same. All that was old was changing forever.

The sun outside ignited like no other day before, and the cold mountain was no longer an enemy. It had split completely, laid open to a meadow... permanently. There was an endless summer inside, flowing out into the world like heat from a hearth. The winter of evil was dying. The world of death was done. The earth was now alive again!

And from the lodge into that golden day, the children, all the children - as children were meant to be in the beginning - ran through the grass and flowers outside, whole, and past the opening of the mountain to play.

Their crutches and blindness, disease, and pain were left in a small lodge, forgotten forever...

...and no one needed words to explain to them anymore.

Craig Smith
02-25-09

AFTERWORDS...

The Christ of Christmas

Micah 5:2 "But you, Bethlehem, though you are small among the clans of Judah, out of you will come one who will be ruler over Israel, whose origins are from of old, from ancient times."

Isaiah 52:4-6 "Surely he took up our infirmities and carried our sorrows, yet we considered him stricken by God, smitten by him, and afflicted. But he was pierced for our transgressions; he was crushed for our iniquities; the punishment that brought us peace was upon him, and by his wounds we are healed. We all, like sheep, have gone astray, each of us has turned to his own way; and the LORD has laid on him the iniquity of us all.

Hebrews 1:1 In the past God spoke to our forefathers through the prophets at many times and in various ways, but in these last days he has spoken to us by his Son, whom he appointed heir of all things, and through whom he made the universe. The Son is the radiance of God's glory and the exact representation of his being, sustaining all things by his powerful word. After he had provided purification for sins, he sat down at the right hand of the Majesty in heaven.

I Corinthians 15:3-6 For what I received I passed on to you as of first importance: that Christ died for our sins according to the Scriptures, that he was buried, that he was raised on the third day according to the Scriptures, and that he appeared to Peter, and then to the Twelve. After that, he appeared to more than five hundred of the brothers at the same time, most of whom are still living, though some have fallen asleep.

Romans 3:21-25 But now a righteousness from God, apart from law, has been made known, to which the Law and the Prophets testify. This righteousness from God comes through faith in Jesus Christ to all who believe. There is no difference, for all have sinned and fall short of the glory of God, and are justified freely by his grace through the redemption that came by Christ Jesus. God presented him as a sacrifice of atonement, through faith in his blood.

Hebrews 9:27-28 Just as man is destined to die once, and after that to face judgment, so Christ was sacrificed once to take away the sins of many people.

The Good News

John 3:16-17 For God so loved the world that he gave his one and only Son, that whoever believes in him shall not perish but have eternal life. For God did not send his Son into the world to condemn the world, but to save the world through him.

Ephesians 1:8 For it is by grace you have been saved, through faith — and this not from yourselves, it is the gift of God, not by works, so that no one can boast.

- Christ came to us as He *promised*...

- He died to redeem & restore us, and change our hearts because we cannot do that ourselves.

- He has power over death. He rose from the grave...

- He returned to heaven and left us His Holy Spirit...

- He will come again, judge the living and the dead and *restore creation*...

John 1:4
In Him was life, and that life was the light of all mankind.

Don't wait. Give him your heart today.

Illustrations and Art

COVER: Photo shop (modified) Main images.
- **Winter holiday background** (Modified) - ID 153472210 Anneleven © (Dreamstime.com License CC0 1.0)
- **Classic white church with steeple near the Mt. Shasta area of California** (Modified) - ID 5507450 © Solasoph (Dreamstime.com License CC0 1.0)

INSIDE: **Newborn Hands Holding** (Modified*) - Pixabay.com Public Domain − Free for commercial use, No attribution required.*

CHRISTMAS BERRIES: **Photo** - Craig Smith

1. A CHRISTMAS SONNET: ***Photo*** *- ID 105771909 Anna Pakutina (Dreamstime.com License CC0 1.0)*

2. UPON ADVENT BORNE: ***Candles in a Greek Orthodox Church*** *- ID 128842387 © Olga Simonova (Dreamstime.com License CC0 1.0)*

3. CAROL OF WINTER: *Photo shop (modified images)*
   - ***Old wooden table and fireplace with warm fire*** *- ID 85411663 © Valentyn75 (Dreamstime.com License CC0 1.0)*
   - ***Pomegranate fruit and wine in the glass***.*ID 82078383 © Ganna Stryzhekin (Dreamstime.com License CC0 1.0)*
   - *Candy's Bible − Photo © Craig Smith*

4. ORNAMENT: ***Earth Ornament*** *- ID 26776471 © Kevin Carden (Dreamstime.com License CC0 1.0)*

5. OF HIM WHO WAS BORN FOR US: *Photo shop (modified images)*
   - **Drum, Fiddle & Whistle** -PhotoID 37656371 © Mrtobin *(Dreamstime.com License CCO 1.0)*
   - **Christmas Table** – *Photo ID 45755131 ©* Fotoschab *(Dreamstime.com License CCO 1.0)*

6. CHRISTMAS GRACE: **Antique Christmas Card: Box of Holly 1907** – *Public Domain, Olddesignshop.com*

7. WINTERS CAROL: **Yellow crocuses growing among snow** - *Photo 113392201 ©* Physyk *(Dreamstime.com License CCO 1.0)*

8. CHRISTMAS NATION: **Christmas Eve at Mount Vernon** – Jean Leon Gerome Ferris, *XoaX.NET Public Domain Images.*

9. KEEPING CHRISTMAS: **Little girl praying in the church in in the rays of the sun** - *ID 170975436 ©* Manifeesto *(Dreamstime.com License CCO 1.0)*

10. THE PRAYER OF THE GLEN:
    - **Saint Bridget of Ireland. Colour lithograph**: *This file comes from Wellcome Images, a website operated by Wellcome Trust, a global charitable foundation based in the United Kingdom, licensed under the Wikimedia Creative Commons Attribution 4.0 International*
    - **The Bard -** John Hall (1784 - *www.metmuseum.org, (CCO Public Domain)*

11. CHRISTMAS COMES BUT ONCE A YEAR: **Couple Walking Through the Snow** - Anna Whelan Betts, *wellcomecollection.org/image/V0039050.jpg, Creative Commons Attribution (CC BY 4.0) terms and conditions.*

12. CHANTONS NOEL: **Scenic view to the Eiffel tower on a day with heavy snow** - *Photo 129983852 © Ekaterina Pokrovsky (Dreamstime.com License CCO 1.0)*

13. A SEASON SILENT: **See Cover Photo**

14. OPLATKI: **Picture of Oplatki being shared** *(Modified) - http://www.poloniasf.org/english/images, (Public Domain Image)*

15. BY YOUR LEAVE TO GO ACROSS THE SEA: **Sailing ship & Stormy Sky**, *Photo ID56151730 © Alexander Lvov (Dreamstime.com License CCO 1.0)*

16. THE DAY YOU CAME: **Corcovado Mountain with Christ the Redeemer Statue** - *Photo ID42510184 © Dabldy (Dreamstime.com License CCO 1.0)*

17. DRIVING TO CHRISTMAS: **Car rides in the winter night** - *ID143734642 © Juri Bizgajmer (Dreamstime.com License CCO 1.0)*

18. NOSTRI SALVATORI: **Manger with Shepherds and Maji** - *Craig Smith, Photo ©*

19. THROUGH THE WINTER OF THE WORLD: **Lonely Woman Looking at Snowfall Through Window** - *ID 59423154 © Robsonphoto 2011 (Dreamstime.com License CCO 1.0)*

20. HAIKU: (Plate) **Pine Tree** – *ID 1489795 © Jetfoto (Dreamstime.com License CCO 1.0)* (Background) **Snow Mountain Zao** - *ID 96742578 © Jannoon028 (Dreamstime.com License CCO 1.0)*

21. THE FINAL WORD: **Praying Hand (modified)** *Photo ID 161252528 © Chumphon Whangchom Dreamstime.com (Dreamstime.com License CCO 1.0)*

About the Author

Craig D. Smith currently lives in Portland, Oregon.

Book of Christmas is his second book of original poetry, also including one short story, all focused around the meaning of Christmas.

His other works include:

Midnight Pieces, a book of personal poetry from over the years including an original short story.

Within the Fire of Evening, a collection of his own imaginative Science Fiction stories authored in a more classical style.

Everyman's War, a book based upon his father's experiences in WWII. He also wrote the screenplay for the award-winning film by the same name.

Other Works by Craig D. Smith
AVAILABLE ON AMAZON.COM

Everyman's War
The Book

"Taut, lean, direct, unadorned, stunningly readable, this story of courage and love quietly becomes the Human Story of Courage and Love. I finished the last pages, thanked the Coherent Mercy for putting me in this bruised and blessed world, and called my dad."
~Brian Doyle, author of
Thirsty for the Joy:
Australian & American Voice

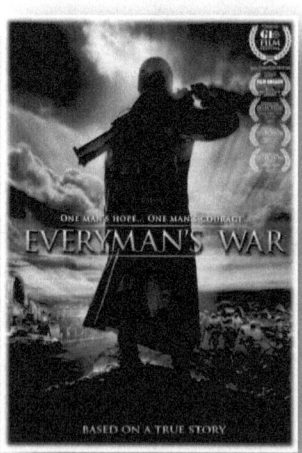

Everyman's War
The Film'
(Now on DVD / Blueray)
Winner G.I. Film Festival'

One man's hope...
One man's courage...
Everyman's War.

"If I could package the mission of the GI Film Festival into one two-hour film, it would be
EVERYMAN'S WAR"
~Brandon L. Millet ~
President G.I. Film Festival 2008

Within the Fire of Evening

"Science-fiction with a heart. It holds the glow of a warm, comforting, eerily familiar future. You will be taken to the stars...You will be taken through time. And woven through it all is a haunting yet uplifting nostalgia for days long past. The settings vary, the humanity doesn't. Here are nine tales that leave you with a yearning, "if only..."

~John Olsen, author of
The Crystal Screen

Midnight Pieces

Twenty poems and one short story. A collection of personal poetry from over the years plus an engaging short story.

*"For those who encourage...
For those who edify...
For those who inspire...
And for those who know midnights..."*

Craig D. Smith